D1586448

Note to parents, carers and teachers

Read it yourself is a series of modern stories, favourite characters and traditional tales written in a simple way for children who are learning to read. The books can be read independently or as part of a guided reading session.

Each book is carefully structured to include many high-frequency words vital for first reading. The sentences on each page are supported closely by pictures to help with understanding, and to offer lively details to talk about.

The books are graded into four levels that progressively introduce wider vocabulary and longer stories as a reader's ability and confidence grows.

Ideas for use

- Ask how your child would like to approach reading at this stage. Would he prefer to hear you read the story first, or would he like to read the story to you and see how he gets on?

- Help him to sound out any words he does not know.

- Developing readers can be concentrating so hard on the words that they sometimes don't fully grasp the meaning of what they're reading. Answering the puzzle questions on pages 46 and 47 will help with understanding.

For more information and advice on Read it yourself and book banding, visit www.ladybird.com/readityourself

Book Band 8

Level 3 is ideal for children who are developing reading confidence and stamina, and who are eager to read longer stories with a wider vocabulary.

Special features:

Detailed pictures for added interest and discussion

Wider vocabulary, reinforced through repetition

Bushy Fandango was taking her submarine down under Potion Ocean. So Poppet stowed away on the submarine.

Longer sentences

Simple story structure

Captain Buck was out there. He wanted to take over Bushy's submarine and he was throwing things at the submarine to make it stop.

CRASH!

CRASH!

Educational Consultant: Geraldine Taylor
Book Banding Consultant: Kate Ruttle

A catalogue record for this book is available from the British Library

This edition published by Ladybird Books Ltd 2013
80 Strand, London, WC2R 0RL
A Penguin Company

001

Ladybird, Read It Yourself and the Ladybird Logo are registered or
unregistered trademarks of Ladybird Books Limited.

ISBN: 978-0-72327-359-2

Printed in China

Poppet
Stows Away

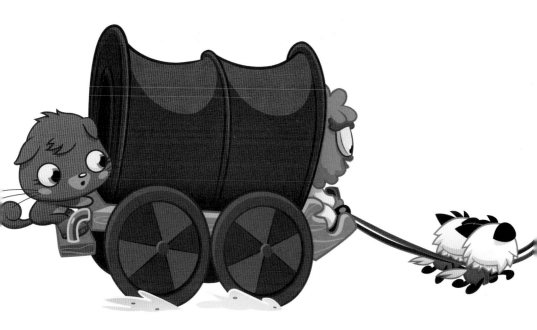

Written by Ronne Randall
Illustrated by Lea Wade

One day, Poppet looked out and saw the explorer Bushy Fandango. Bushy was going away again, this time to explore under the ocean.

Poppet wanted to go exploring with Bushy.

"If I ask to go, too, Bushy Fandango will just say no," Poppet thought. "I'll have to stow away."

Potion Ocean

Bushy Fandango was taking her submarine down under Potion Ocean. So Poppet stowed away on the submarine.

Bushy was surprised to see Poppet.
"You have stowed away!" she said.
"You could get hurt!"

"I'm all right," said Poppet.
"I just want to go exploring with you."

All at once there was a CRASH!

Poppet looked out of the submarine to see what was going on.

Captain Buck was out there.
He wanted to take over Bushy's
submarine and he was throwing
things at the submarine to make
it stop.

CRASH!

CRASH!

Bushy was surprised to see Captain Buck. "I thought he was my friend!" she said.

"This is not like him at all!" said Poppet.

"Dr Strangeglove must have put a spell on him," said Bushy.

"What can we do?" asked Poppet.

"We must stop Captain Buck hurting my submarine," said Bushy. "Let's see if we can make him go away."

20

But Captain Buck kept throwing
things at the submarine.

"We must make him stop!"
said Bushy. "But how?"

"I have an idea," said Poppet. "We can put out a signal asking for help!"

"What a good idea, Poppet!" cried Bushy. "Let's do it right now!"

24

So Bushy put out a signal and
Octo came to help right away.

Octo sprayed water at the captain, but it was no help.

Then Octo's friends Myrtle and Gail came to see if they could help.

"We'll do what we can to stop the captain," they said.

But Myrtle and Gail couldn't make Captain Buck stop! He sprayed Toad Soda at the submarine.

"Not Toad Soda!" cried Bushy.

Then Octo had an idea. He sprayed Toad Soda back at Captain Buck. The spray of Toad Soda surprised Captain Buck so much that all at once he was all right again.

"Arrr, Dr Strangeglove put me under a spell," he said. "I couldn't help what I did. I am very sorry."

"Arrr, how can I make it up to you?" Captain Buck asked Bushy.

"You can help us look for a Black Pearl under Potion Ocean," said Bushy.

"Aye aye!" said Captain Buck. "Let's go!"

The captain made the submarine all right again. Then they all went down under the water to look for the Black Pearl.

"Look over there!" said Captain Buck.

"A Black Pearl!" said Bushy. "But Cali the Valley Mermaid is there, too, and she won't let us take it."

"I have another idea!" said Poppet.

Poppet made a coffee.

"Coffee!" said Cali the Valley Mermaid. "I must have it!"

She came over for the coffee, and Bushy could now take the Black Pearl. Bushy was very happy.

"Poppet, you helped me to get the Black Pearl," said Bushy. "Will you come exploring with me again another day? You won't have to stow away this time!"

"Yes," said Poppet. Now she was very happy, too!

How much do you remember about the story of Moshi Monsters: Poppet Stows Away? Answer these questions and find out!

- **Where is Bushy Fandango going exploring?**

- **Where does Poppet stow away?**

- **Who attacks the submarine?**

- **Who comes to help Poppet and Bushy?**

- **What is Bushy looking for under Potion Ocean?**

- **How does Poppet get Cali the Valley Mermaid to let them take the Black Pearl?**

Look at the different story sentences and match them to the characters who said them.

"Arrr, how can I make it up to you?"

"Coffee! I must have it!"

"We'll do what we can to stop the captain."

"I'm all right, I just want to go exploring with you."

"We must stop Captain Buck hurting my submarine."

Read it yourself with Ladybird

Tick the books you've read!

For more confident readers who can read simple stories with help.

Level 3

 YOU won't like this present as much as I DO!

 The Elves and the Shoemaker

☐ ☐

 Hansel and Gretel

 Harry and the Bucketful of Dinosaurs

 Jack and the Beanstalk

 Furi on Music Island

 Poppet Stows Away

 Rapunzel

 The Red Knight

☐ ☐ ☐ ☐ ☐ ☐ ☐

Longer stories for more independent, fluent readers.

Level 4

 I am Inventing an INVENTION

 Harry and the Dinosaurs United

☐ ☐

 Heidi

 Katsuma and the Art Thief

 Luvli and the Glump-a-tron

 The Pied Piper of Hamelin

 Sam and the Robots

 Snow White and the Seven Dwarfs

 The Wizard of Oz

☐ ☐ ☐ ☐ ☐ ☐ ☐